# TALES OF YESTERYEAR:
# *Lifetimes of Whimsy*

RYAN EHRHARDT

# Contents

# Prologue

The world is a big, fascinating place full of interesting, complex individuals. Hi, I'm Ryan and these are some of my favorite tales of life. Not my life. My life isn't that interesting, but I know interesting people. These are a compilation of tales from the most interesting people I've known, as told by me, someone who wasn't there and is just regurgitating things people told me. This first tale is about an intrepid man, a true titan of industry, and his struggle to deal with a younger, more talented person coming to replace him. This tale is called, "Fieri's Fury: The Battle for Flavortown".

# Fieri's Fury: The Battle for Flavortown

Steve was just an ordinary guy who had big dreams of big flavors. He loved the food network. He'd watch it all day, admiring the skills of these top chefs, often ending in him attempting to recreate the bold flavors he had seen on TV. However, every time he tried he fell flat; his flavors just weren't bold enough. So he'd wallow in his self pity while shame eating his regularly flavored olive loaf. He thought his dreams would never come to fruition.

But one day, he woke up and could just sense something was different. He didn't know what came over him, but he just went straight to the kitchen and started flambéing a pork chop. The seasonings were second nature: paprika, cumin, garlic pepper, basil, heck, even a little cayenne. It didn't matter if conventional wisdom dictated the flavors paired well together, because he could balance anything. And if he knew anything, it's that flavor creation was all about balance.

Finally, Steve was finished. It was time for the taste test. He cut into the pork chop and it was perfect, medium rare. He tasted it, and the texture from the sear marks was excellent. There was some kick, but not too much. And most importantly, every flavor was perfectly balanced. The verdict: bold flavors. These were the boldest flavors he had ever tasted.

Overcome with glee from his newfound abilities, Steve quickly whipped up some more bold flavors and went door to door in his 4-story apartment building insisting everyone taste his flavors. And sure enough, without fail, every person who experienced Steve's flavors said, "Wow, did you create these flavors? They're incredibly bold!"

Steve understood that he needed to share his flavors with the world, as they were just too bold to keep to himself, not to mention that he had always believed that it was his life's calling to create bold flavors. So, he opened up a restaurant, a swank little joint in downtown Chicago, home to the boldest flavors either side of the Mason-Dixon. Every patron who dined on his delicious dishes left his restaurant in awe of the boldness of his flavors. He would become known around the world as "Big Flavor Steve."

Big Flavor Steve's flavor creation abilities were unparalleled. He possessed the ability to make bold flavors that many could never dream of. Everyone he met said his food was "out of bounds" and "a one way ticket to flavortown." He became so beloved that the people eventually anointed him "Mayor of Flavortown." However, his powers came at a cost, for in this world there must be balance. For all the good flavors he's created, he's left an especially bad taste in one person's mouth: Guy Fieri. Upon hearing that he's been usurped of his title as "Mayor of Flavortown," he becomes enraged and leads an angry mob of celebrity chefs to storm Big Flavor Steve's kitchen. Every celebrity chef under the sun is in this mob: Alex Guarnaschelli, Robert Irvine, Bobby Flay, Maneet Chauhan, and, of course, Gordon motherfuckin' Ramsey. They were his top sous-rioters.

At 6:48 they arrived at the kitchen to organize and create a battle plan. It got heated as they deliberated. Each personality as bold as the flavors they create, tensions were bound to boil over like water in an unwatched pot. But finally, as a true leader would, Guy Fieri took command of the room. "SILENCE," he stated forcefully, yet not in a yell-y kind of way, as a true leader would. "Gather 'round gang, here's what we're gonna do…" and he proceeded to tell them his plan. I don't even think I need to mention they were very receptive. They all respect his bold flavors.

At 7:03 pm they began their attack. The chefs hurled meats, seasonings, and all sorts of bold flavors at Big Flavor Steve. Meatballs, cayenne, basil, Worcestershire sauce, cumin, ham sandwiches, the list goes on and on. But their assault was no match for Steve's skills. Everything they threw at him he caught and threw into a pot and turned into his finest creation yet. It didn't have a name because no one had ever had the ability to create such bold flavors. Big Flavor Steve was only getting stronger.

In hindsight they probably should have seen this coming. Seven o'clock is the start of the dinner rush. It's when he's at his strongest and his flavors reach peak boldness. But Guy Fieri had one last trick up the sleeve of his patented bowling shirt: Donkey Sauce. He hurled a vial of that sweet nectar straight at Big Flavor Steve, and without thinking he poured the vial into the pot thinking there was no way he couldn't balance the flavors. But he couldn't do it. The sweet and the sour, the bitter and the spice, it was all off. There was no balance. The Donkey Sauce was too gangster, its flavors too bold. Big Flavor Steve just left Flavortown. Dejected, Big Flavor Steve left the kitchen and swore off bold flavor creation for the remainder of his days, surrendering the title of Mayor of Flavortown back to Guy Fieri. Henceforth, he was once again known simply as Steve.

It was a victory for Guy Fieri. His flavors were too bold for even a superhuman flavor creator, yet something about the situation felt hollow. It felt as though he may have seen himself become the villain. He could sense that he had removed a beautiful and steadying societal force from this world, and now there was a lack of balance. And if there's one thing a Mayor of Flavortown knows about, it's balance.

But what was done was done. He went back to work, looking for America's greatest diners, drive-ins, and dives. But his search was painful. Everywhere he went he was accosted by fellow flavor creators, knowing what flavors he had taken from this world.

At a diner in Memphis, Tennessee, he had a shrimp po' boy so good he could have sworn he'd died and gone to New Orleans. With that loveable, infectious Fieri flare, he turned to the chef and proclaimed, "Dude, that was out of bounds!"

The restaurateur dismissively replied, "No, what was out of bounds was you hurling that vile of Donkey Sauce at Big Flavor Steve. You killed his spirit by crippling his bold flavors. You need to understand that his achievements in flavor don't detract from what you've accomplished."

"Yeah, I'm beginning to see that. I just haven't felt whole since the Battle for Flavortown," said the Mayor of Flavortown.

The restaurateur, now feeling sorry for Guy and understanding the burden he carries with him on a day-to-day basis, simply said, "You know what you have to do."

Nodding his head in agreement, Guy responded, "I know," and he darted out of the kitchen, got in his bitchin' Camaro and drove to Steve's place. All along the way, he rehearsed what he was going to say, but he just couldn't find the words. You'd think he would have, considering it was an 8 hour drive, but it was just so hard to describe how profoundly remorseful he was for ridding the world of those angelic flavors.

Finally he arrived at Steve's dank studio apartment. Steve had fallen on significant economic hardship since surrendering the title of Mayor of Flavortown. He knocked on Steve's door for at least 17 minutes. And I mean 17 consecutive minutes of non-stop knocking. I had no idea that it was possible to have that level of persistence. Can you imagine the knuckle pain? Anyway, he knew Steve had to be in there because, through his knocking, Mr. Fieri heard the microwave start and finish, and he heard the TV turn on. Finally, Steve defeatedly cries out, "Fine, come in."

What Guy Fieri sees when he walks in rocks him to his core: Steve in his underpants, eating a hot pocket, the most perfectly prepared hot pocket of all time. He really had sworn off bold flavors. He wouldn't even let himself indulge in his own flavors. Guy looks at the TV and sees The Food Network. Clearly Steve missed his flavors. After processing this, Guy said, "Hey man…"

Steve's head whipped around to see none other than the Mayor of Flavortown. Panicked, he fumbled for his remote, trying to turn off the TV as quickly as possible like he had been caught watching porn, because in a way, he had. He hastily and bitterly said to Guy, "What do you want?"

"I wanted to tell you how sorry I am," Guy responded. "I was wrong to be so jealous of your bold flavors. I got so caught up with trying to have the boldest flavors that I didn't appreciate the boldness of your flavors, the balance of your dishes. All I could think about was the fact that I had been usurped of my title as Mayor of Flavortown."

Now fighting through the tears welling up in his eyes, in a whimpery, choked-up tone, Steve said, "You don't get it man. I never cared about titles. I didn't ask for these powers, I didn't ask for that plane to fly over the Chernobyl plant…"

An inquisitive Guy questioned, "Really? Is that how you got your flavors?"

"I'm pretty sure. I don't know what else it would be," Steve replied. "But seriously though, I never asked for any of this. I wanted to use my powers for good. I wanted to bring people joy and satiation, and most importantly, bold flavors."

"I know, I know," a remorseful Guy retorted, "I lost sight of what truly matters in life: bold flavors. And if you can bring more bold, balanced flavors into the world, then I shouldn't stop you. I came here to ask you to return to the kitchen. I came here..." Guy paused, understanding the gravity of what he was about to say. "I came here to crown you Mayor of Flavortown, Big Flavor Steve."

Flabbergasted by the gesture, Steve said, "Woah. That fake title is like the only thing you care about in this world. I couldn't..."

"You can and you will," interjected Guy Fieri. "And you'll be needing this."

He hands Big Flavor Steve a bowling shirt and some back-of-the-head Oakley's. "What's all this?" Big Flavor Steve asked.

Guy Fieri, coyly chuckling to himself, said "Your uniform son. If you're gonna be the Mayor of Flavortown, you're gonna need to look like the Mayor of Flavortown."

Big Flavor Steve was still teary eyed, but he now had different tears: tears of joy. "Wow, I can't thank you enough Mr. Fieri. This is the kindest thing anyone's done for me. I'm gonna cherish these Oakley's."

"Don't mention it," Guy FIeri said, sounding like a proud dad getting his son his pair of Oakley's. "And my friends don't call me Mr. Fieri, they call me host of the Food Network's Diners, Drive-ins and Dives, Guy fieri."

With a gleeful, youthful, yet still vaguely submissive exuberance, Big Flavor Steve said "You got it, host of the Food Network's Diners, Drive-ins and Dives, Guy fieri." Then they jumped in the air and high-fived, ya know, like what you'd see on one of those posters captioned, "Friendship".

After that they went their separate, flavorful ways. Big Flavor Steve went back to making the biggest, boldest flavors known to man, and Guy Fieri continued making his own damn fine flavors. They were never envious of another man's flavors again, and spent the rest of their days creating and appreciating bold flavors.

The end.

# SEGUE 1

I know right, Guy Fieri always seemed so chill. You'd have never thought he'd be that jealous of another man's flavors. But hey, you live and you learn, and I think the OG mayor of Flavortown himself learned a thing or two about humility. And ya know what, I think that's just gangster. The next tale on the docket is a pretty sharp left turn from this one, quite a bit edgier, and dare I say, more thought provoking. This next story tells the tale of two gym bros and how their quest for pussy leads them to a woman who would change their lives forever. This is the tale of Dirk, Chad, and the Schlong Shaman.

# Dirk, Chad, and the Schlong Shaman.

> Warning: The following contains graphic
> douchebaggery. Reader's discretion is advised.

Dirk and Chad were two quintessential bros. Their entire lives revolved around growing their muscles, then looking at their muscles, and then, as they liked to say, "poundin' puss". They spent many of their waking hours in the gym, where they both boasted a variety of cut-off t-shirts featuring statements like "No Days Off", and "No Pain, No Gain", which obviously were super cool. Their favorite shirt said "Every Day is Leg Day", though in a twist of irony, they consistently skipped leg day. Instead they opted to stand in the mirror and do curls for several hours, until they got what was known as "that crazy pump". They would stand there in the mirror staring at each other's sick bi-s in admiration, while slowly moving the weights over their crotch, which was concealing erections they affectionately referred to as "penis pumps".

After getting that stupid pump, that crazy pump, that bonkers pump, it was off to the locker room, where the next 30 to 60 minutes were spent meticulously crafting pictures to post on "the gram". For reasons neither of them understood, they were always super turned on after all of this. Their post workout penis pumps were always fully torqued every time they analyzed each other's sweaty, shirtless bodies. It was after this that they went out to smash some snatch.

And corral the cooch they did. They were some of the most successful taco stuffers in the game. They were known by all who wore Axe body spray. One of the traits that made them so legendary on the slit slayin' scene was their innovation. They believed nothing was off-limits, which made anything possible. Their most notorious pick-up spot was the National Suicide Prevention Hotline. Now, you may be thinking to yourself that this is morally reprehensible behavior or that this is just simply a really ineffective way to get laid. Well, to you they would simply say that you have no game, and that you are, quote, "a punk ass, pussy bitch who probably doesn't even get that good puss." They claimed that it was a great way to, quote, "score some sympathy snatch", and to the disappointment of all the haters/decent people, all about perspective on that one, the results suggested their claim was true. Just shockingly accurate.

But what really gave the pair such a prodigious, poon-tang pulling pedigree was just that, they were a pair. The fact that the two rolled as a package deal opened them up to a world of possibilities. When they started working it, they knew they'd finish the job. There was never a time when one of them wasn't being totally awesome. Ya know, flexing, talking about their muscles, saying things like she "fills out them jeans just right," asking if she has any hot friends, etc. Just cool guy stuff.

Then they'd nail 'em as a duo. They absolutely loved it. They loved it so much that there were times when they couldn't even do it without the other one there. Dirk and Chad's top position was the Eiffel Tower. They would get in their positions, Dirk in front and Chad in back, and they would lock their hands up top while staring into each other's eyes, getting lost in the moment and just appreciating one another. They were perfectly in-sync, becoming one, but they insisted it was, quote, "in a totally non-gay way." They would dreamily gaze directly into each other's soul while repeatedly whispering the phrase, "no homo."

Then, one day, one fateful day, they were out browsin' the boulevards for bodacious babes, when they saw the most marvelous mass of mammaries in memory. She was exquisite, wonderful, bonerific. She was the paragon of pussy, the Schlong Shaman.

When they approached her, they quickly found that this wasn't your typical girl. No, she, like Dirk and Chad, was a douche. She started working game on them. They didn't know how to react. She started negging them. The two of them couldn't take it. That was their thing. They were the kings of dinging a girl's self-esteem just enough to make her lower her standards. Now someone had the audacity to do the same thing to them? They were incensed.

Dirk, suddenly a Picky-Pete about who pulls his pecker, said, "What are you, some sort of wanker weasel? Trying to weasel your way into some wanker?"

Stunned, and frankly irritated by this turn of events, the Schlong Shaman retorted, "What, you don't want this? What are you, a couple of weasel wankers?"

"Woah woah woah!" cried Chad, incensed by the comment. "Are you suggesting I rub off rodents?"

Baffled, and frankly even more irritated by the stupidity she was just confronted with, the Schlong Shaman said, "What? No. What the...what the fuck? No you fucking moron. Weasel is a euphemism for dick you dilhole."

Now a little overly defensive, Dirk, puffing out his chest like a real cool guy, responded, "Yo, I'm not gay. The fuck are you talking about? I'm no homo."

"Wow, I didn't know homosexuality offended you so much," accosted the Schlong Shaman, who just pretended she hadn't also said something wildly homophobic out of frustration.

Now more defensive, Chad said, "I don't hate homos. I'm totally cool with homos. In fact…"

The next moment, like always, the two were perfectly in sync. Dirk and Chad turn to face each other and slowly move in towards one another to kiss. At first they're hesitant, but as the moments pass they give into their passion, their long repressed homoerotic lust for one another, likely developed from all those days of skipping legs to watch each other do curls in cut off t-shirts. Moments turned into seconds, and seconds turned into minutes, and eventually a half-hour. And for some the reason the Schlong Shaman just stood there, watching these two bros tongue-fuck each other for thirty consecutive minutes.

When they finally come up for air, a heavy breathing Dirk stood back up straight and re-postured himself like the total bro he is. In a winded voice, he says, "Good shit bro, that was some good shit. No homo."

Chad, in a similar manner, responded, "Yeah bro, that was some good tongue, no homo."

"Yeah bro, you too. No wonder so much of that pussy comes back for seconds. You made me a little hard too, no homo." Dirk responded.

"Yeah bro, I'm hard too," Chad responded. Now with his shoulders slouching just a bit and with just a hint of vulnerability in his voice, Chad shyly stated, "and I guess, if I'm being totally honest, a little homo."

Dirk, predictably assuming a similar posture, since it was pretty clear from the beginning these two were soulmates, with a similar vulnerability said, "Yeah bro, I guess I also had a little homo. I never felt that way with anyone before." Suddenly reverting back to his macho persona, Dirk defensively and expeditiously proclaimed, "But I don't think it means anything. We're still bros, bro. I still like poundin' puss bro. I'm all about slaying snatch yo. Gotta hound a ho, ya know. It's all this bitch's fault for making us think we're homos."

Now munching pretzels for some reason, the Schlong Shaman, befuddled by so much of what's transpired, stated, "What are you talking about? I didn't make you gay. And if you don't exclusively like dudes, you're not gay, you're bisexual. It means you like bros and hos."

Chad, in his still vulnerable state, said, "Ya know bro, I think she's right. Like, don't get me wrong, I still love crushing cooch and blasting beaver, but it's always better with you, for so many reasons. I'm more confident on the mount because I know you can pick up the slack if I have an off day. I always think about you in graphic, sexual scenarios and it's exciting to play them out in real life. And when you're not around, there's a massive gaping hole in my life."

Almost moved to tears by the candor and sentiment of his bro, Dirk said, "Yeah bro, I know what you mean. I'm like rock hard when you curl in your cut-off. And, if you'll have me, I'd like to make a new gaping hole in your life...with my penis."

Now completely moved to tears, Chad joyously cried out, "Yes! Yes! A thousand times yes!" With a sudden shift in tone to one that's more uncertain and panicky, Chad asked, "But what about the bros? What will we tell the dudes?"

Putting on a brave face, Dirk replied, "I don't know, but we'll figure it out. They should understand. They're our bros, bro. Plus, I think Dak and Dom like each other. They shower together all the time."

Now a little excited, the Schlong Shaman giddily inquired, "Damn, where is this house?" And that's the last we hear from her for a while. We'll circle back though.

Now back at the house, Dirk and Chad decide to just rip off the band-aid. They called a house meeting with the ceremonial shaking of the empty shaker bottle. Just quintessential bro shit. And as per tradition, each of the bros entered the room shaking empty bottles of their own. Marching to the sound of their own whisks, Brett and Brock enter, followed by Zaine and Shane, and then the aforementioned Dak and Dom. They all gathered around Dirk and Chad, and Brett asked, "Sup bro, why'd you summon us?"

"Guys, we have an announcement," responded Dirk, "Me and Chad are a couple of bi-bros. We like doing gay shit with each other."

"Woah! Bro, woah!" exclaimed Dom, as though this concept was completely foreign to him.

"Listen," said Chad, in a patient yet commanding tone, "I know it's a lot bros, but we're still the same bros, bros. We still love foraging bush, but sometimes we wouldn't mind some dude bush."

Dak, currently rubbing Dom while whispering no homo, says, "Bro. That's like crazy yo. How are you even gay? The only gays I know are like super gay."

Then, from the shadows, who else would appear but the Schlong Shaman, and she was in a preaching kind of mood. "Listen up bitches," the Shaman commandingly dictated to the bros. "It's very common to have homoerotic thoughts. Lots of people have them and act on them. And you shouldn't say things like someone is super gay. That implies that there is a right and wrong way to be who you are. There are plenty of people out there who don't neatly fit into the stereotypes they're expected to conform to. Heck, I don't "look" like a lesbian, but sometimes I'll use my girl Suze as a make-shift muff-muzzle."

"You know about muff-muzzles?" asked Dirk.

"Of course, I invented that shit," the Shaman replied.

"Nice," said an impressed Chad.

"How did you even get here," inquired Dirk. "We didn't tell you where the house was. The story just abruptly stopped."

She replied, "Chad left his wallet at the bar and it for some reason had his address taped to it."

"It's so I don't forget where I live," Chad bluntly replied.

Once again irritated by this bro's stupidity, the Schlong Shaman replied, "What the fuck? Aren't you like 25? How could you forget your address? Did you hit your or something?"

"Ooh, a quarter," replied Chad.

Regaining that manhood messiah mojo and powering past whatever that was, the Shaman said, "Anyway, lots of people think and do those things and it's totally normal."

Dom, now taking a similar tone that Dirk and Chad had earlier, said to Dak, "Ya know bro, she might have a point. I'm like rock hard from you rubbing me."

Dak, in that same tone, replied, "Yeah bro, rubbing you makes me real hard. And when we shower together, I always cum."

"I know, I know," Dom retorted. "It made the shower real crusty and a lot less slippery. You make me feel safer."

The Schlong Shaman, equal parts grossed out by the state of the shower, turned on by the thought of them showering, and annoyed by how incredibly repetitive this shit had gotten, suddenly had an epiphany. Turning to Chad, she said, "Chad, did you slip in the shower?"

Chad, in that stupid fuckin voice, replied, "I used to all the time, but then it got real crusty." I know, everything Chad is painful, but he's so integral to this story.

All the goofy Chad shit aside, there was still a part of the Schlong Shaman that couldn't help being touched by all the love that had been discovered before her very eyes. But her job was not done yet. The manhood messiah still had to shepherd another to enlightenment. Brett, one of the bros who entered initially, in case you forgot, said, "Well I don't get it. Why don't I ever think gay shit? Am I not normal?"

The Schlong Shaman, with all her wisdom and without any hesitation, responded, "That's normal too. It's all normal, or weird, or whatever. It doesn't matter. We don't choose to feel what we feel, we just feel. Love and sexuality are incredibly abstract concepts and completely unquantifiable. They baffle the even brightest of minds and warm even the coldest of hearts. People spend their whole lives searching for their own personal answers, and sometimes, they're lucky enough to find their answer. They don't know how they got there, but they're sure glad they made it. Now one of you homos get over here. This pussy ain't gonna eat itself."

And gobble gash they did. But no longer was their goal to prove their bro-y-ness, but rather because they simply had a passion for cunnilingus, or munching minge as it were. Such was the way now for Dirk and Chad, as that was the day they had their bro-lightening.

And so it was that the Schlong Shaman was the spiritual guide for these bros on their journey to self-discovery. All the bros learned to accept that human sexuality is a highly complex entity with no simple explanations, and that feeling ashamed of their feelings was the only thing to be ashamed of. Except Zaine and Shane, who were major assholes and never grew as people. For years after this, the Schlong Shaman would bring her other douchey friends, Carol and Diane, over to "The Bone Zone" for some of the most vulgar, depraved orgies this world has ever known, until everyone turned 30. At that point every participant agreed that they were too old and went out and scored some 18 year olds, because of course they did.

Though their journey to self-discovery was a long one, Dirk and Chad made it. Along the way they not only discovered what was in their hearts, but also helped their friends find what was in theirs. The remainder of their days were great, as they all lived amorously ever after.

The end.

# SEGUE 2

Well, wasn't that surprisingly heart warming? A group of people who are objectively the worst, not only becoming better people, but opening themselves up to the true happiness that had been in front of them their whole lives. The next story I intend to tell you follows protagonists on a very different journey, but a journey to self-fulfillment nonetheless. This next story tells the tale of two inseparable friends and jammin' partners, and the trials and tribulations they face as they attempt to fill out their band. This is "Drumming Up Controversy".

# Drumming Up Controversy

J ake and Austin had been inseparable for as long as they could remember. Ever since they were young, they had been best friends, and it was a mutual love of music that brought them together. Jake loved the guitar and Austin loved the bass. They played together all the time and got really good. They also just meshed really well together. They were each the yin to the other's yang. With Jake on guitar and Austin on bass, the only thing they were missing was a little percussion.

One day they met a guy that everyone called Dan the Drummer, ya know, because his name's Dan and he's a drummer. They really hit it off and invited Dan over for a jam sesh. It went great. They completed each other. Dan was the peanut butter to Jake and Austin's jelly, the apple to their pie, the shrimp to their grits. You get it, they were good together. Because it went so well, they decided to start making their jam seshes a regular thing. Friday night at 7p.m. was henceforth known as jammin' time. For 8 straight weeks they rock out like none other, jammin' their little hearts out. They even started writing some music of their own. It was effortless, like they'd been doing it all their life.

Then, on the 9th week, Dan didn't show up. Jake and Austin were flummoxed. They had no idea where Dan was. It wasn't like him to miss a jam sesh, as he'd shown up the previous 8 weeks. Concerned, they went to Dan's house to see what was the matter, and from his basement arose such a clatter. Sounds of snares and symbols danced in their heads, with relief that Dan wasn't dead. They're a very dramatic bunch. Hypochondriacs too. Jake has WebMD bookmarked on his computer. But that's neither here nor there. The concerned friends then proceeded to knock on his door. Then again and again and again. After minutes without an answer, Jake and Austin decided to dash in. They make their way to the basement and find that Dan was jammin' with another man.

"Dan!" Jake cried.

"How could you!" Austin implored.

"Huh?" responded Dan, with great confusion.

"Don't 'Huh' me mister!" Jake retorted with a palpable disappointed indignation, the caliber of which that's typically only found in stereotypically Catholic and Jewish mothers. "You know what you did," Jake implored.

"Jammin' with another man!" Austin interjected, with a similar indignation.

Jake then responded to Austin, saying, "Hey, cool it man. Just let me talk. Let's not gang up on him."

"Alright, alright…" Austin submissively replied.

Now more confused, Dan replied with a vaguely dismissive gesture in their direction, "I don't know what it is you two have going on there, but I don't see what the big deal is here. Who cares who I jam with?"

"We do!" Austin cried out with a slight feebleness in his voice that could only mean he was on the verge of tears.

Jake gave Austin a furrowed look that was kind of a hybrid between contempt and concern, but just wound up looking grossed out. With an annoyed, commanding tone he tells Austin, "Dude, seriously, keep it together."

"My bad…" Austin feebly replied.

Then, seemingly unabashed by this whole Austin situation, Jake's glare darts back over to Dan, quickly returning to that aforementioned indignation. "We were a band, Dan. How could you just cheat on us with this floozy guitarist," accosted Jake.

Now on the defensive, Dan replied, "Hey man, we never said we were exclusive. I thought we were just jammin', having a good time. So what if I'm jammin' with Steve?"

Oh yeah, that guitarist Dan got caught with is named Steve. That's not really relevant, I just thought I'd clear up any confusion. Anyway, needless to say Jake did not appreciate that response. His eyes were expressive eyes, and in that moment they only expressed one thing: hurt. In a solemn, resigned, yet still disappointed tone, he replied, "Wow. We've been jammin' for 8 weeks. This was supposed to be our 9th consecutive week of jammin'. We made music together, man. Good music. Maybe not radio good, but it was SoundCloud good. We weren't a band, huh? Well, if all of that meant nothing to you, I guess we're done here." Now wiping a lone tear from his eye like a Native American man witnessing littering, he turns to his somber pal and says, "Let's go, Austin". And they walked up the stairs and out of Dan's life.

With a blank look of solemn disbelief, Dan stared at the stairs from whence they left, with the realization slowly sinking in of what he both had and lost. But he couldn't go back now. He was too stubborn and headstrong. What was done was done. He made his bed, so he laid in it. He was with Steve now. Jake and Austin were but a memory.

For weeks, Dan and Steve jammed, but it wasn't good, not at all. It just didn't seem to work. They tried making music, but it wasn't even SoundCloud good. It was profoundly bad. What they did to music could only be described as a hate crime. But no matter how clear it became that he and Steve weren't a suitable pairing, Dan wouldn't go back to Jake and Austin, because of his aforementioned head strength.

Meanwhile, Jake and Austin stayed up every night, crying into each other's arms about the betrayal of their former bandmate. And it was an aggressive, messy, slobbery, snotty cry. Literally every night for 17 consecutive weeks. They tried recruiting new drummers, but every time they heard the rap of the snare, tears. Every time they heard the crash of the symbol, blubbering. Through their tears they'd pitifully exclaim, "You're not Dan!" They needed Dan back in their lives, but in a weird twist of irony these blubbering messes were just too damn proud to go beg that back-stabbing hussy to rejoin their band.

And that's how it was. Three men without a band, without a sense of belonging, and without the sense of purpose and companionship that accompanies collaborative songwriting. Dan in particular had a rough go of it. At least Jake and Austin had each other. Poor Dan was all alone. He was the loneliest he'd ever been. And his loneliness was exacerbated even further when his tarantula committed suicide. Dan spent so many of his waking hours just sitting, staring out the window while U2 played in the background. With or Without You, I Still Haven't Found What I'm Looking For, All I Want is You, Sunday Bloody Sunday. That last one he actually played after his tarantula killed himself. Boy was that messy.

Then one day, after 19 and a half weeks of looking out the window, Dan says, "I need to get them back." So he spent the next 11 weeks planning a grand gesture to win over Jake and Austin. He ultimately spends $1100 dollars and develops a heart condition from the stress of planning, which he now can't pay for, as the operation was an even $1100.

When he finally went to get them back, Dan arrived at Jake and Austin's house proudly carrying a boombox, because in the end, of course he went with the cliché "Say Anything" scene. But anyway, he held up the boombox and yelled out, "Jake, Austin, I'm sorry! You were right! I was stupid to think our jam seshes were meaningless! I've been lost without you! I have had no one since my tarantula killed himself!"

"Terrence? Terrence the tarantula?" Jake interjected.

"Yeah," Dan replied.

"I'm sorry for your loss. Carry on," Jake called back.

Touched by the sentiment, Dan replied, "Thanks man. It's been tough. I didn't know tarantulas could perform ritualistic disembowelment. But I digress. I just needed you to know that I'm just a drummer, standing in front of some strummers, asking them if they want to jam."

Taking a moment to process everything that just transpired, Jake and Austin gave Dan a good look. A real good look. Finally, after 19 agonizing seconds, Jake replied, "Dan…", pausing again for just a little too long, "let's jam."

Now euphoric, Dan gleefully leapt into the air and shouted, "Yippee!", though he did drop the boombox he was holding. He was so happy though he didn't even notice. Moments later he gets more great news.

Jake calls out, "Hey man, don't even worry about that $1100, we'll pay for your heart surgery!"

To this day people wonder how they knew about the heart condition considering they hadn't had contact for 38 and two-thirds weeks, but many have speculated that they have a special connection because they were twins separated at birth. They assume this because they're identical. The other leading theory was that they were products of the government's cloning program, but that was debunked in the landmark piece, Friedrich et al.

But that's neither here nor there, because they all got their happy ending. The unfillable vacancy in their lives had at last been filled. Finally, after 38 and two-thirds weeks, they were a band again. They all jammed radically ever after.

The end.

# SEGUE 3

A total tearjerker, that one. Gets me everytime. In case you are wondering, yes, they're still a band, yes, they've released several albums, and yes, they've sold some of them, over two dozen actually. Unlike the previous tales, the next story has nothing to do with meaningful human connection. It's about power, deceit, greed, and haggling. Mostly haggling. This next story tells the tale of an ambitious, smooth talking cabby who gets involved with the wrong people working his way up the corporate ladder. This is "Haggle This: A Cash Cabby Confession."

# Haggle This: A Cash Cabby Confession

Clinton Fitzsimmons, who his friends call Clint, was just your typical cabby. He was a friendly guy with little patience for traffic. He didn't live lavishly, but he earned livable wages. However, some would suggest he didn't live lavishly enough, and this would be because he was incredibly cheap.

Clint was well known among all kinds of store owners for his haggling. He was a self taught haggler. He had seen people do it in movies, so he knew it couldn't be that hard. The key was to always pay in cash. He lived his entire life by one mantra, WWTMD: What Would the Mafia Do. The answer every time: offer to pay in cash.

Sal, the owner of Sal's pizza, has many stories of Clint's haggling, and weirdly enough all his attempts seemed ineffective. Every encounter went roughly the same way: Clint would order a pie, then low-ball the price. He would say, "So, I see the Mediterranean is twenty-five dollars." Then he would coyly look from side to side and lean in over the counter and whisper to the clerk, "I could take that off your hands today. I'll pay you twenty dollars, cash."

The cashier would typically respond, "That'll be twenty-five dollars." This guy was wise to this game.

Then Clint would respond, "Alright, so you wanna play hardball, eh?" Then he'd lean in, again looking from side to side, and say, "How about I give you twenty-two dollars, cash."

The cashier responded, "That'll be twenty-five dollars."

Then, Clint would pull out a pillowcase full of pennies and say, "Alright, you drive a hard bargain. I'll pay you twenty-four dollars and 96 cents, cash."

At this point, the exasperated cashier would begrudgingly say, "Fine, whatever. Just go away." And that was how he did it, that was how he won. The haggler haggled again. But it always felt hollow and pointless. Yes, he paid below the asking price, but by only four cents. So much work for so little payout. It was nothing like the movies

It seemed like such a foolproof plan. Offer to pay less money, but do it in cash. Clint even started to become dispirited and lose faith in his haggling abilities. But then, one day, he was giving a cab ride to notorious mobster John Gotti, ya know, as one does, and received the biggest tip he had ever gotten. Ten-thousand dollars, cash. Gotti told Clint to get himself a new cab and that he'd get a sweet deal if he told the dealer he'd pay cash, to which Clint naturally responded, "Trust me, I know all about paying cash."

So Clint went down to the dealer and found his dream cab. It was yellow, it had all of its windows, it was perfect. The asking price was $14,000, but he confidently strolled right into the dealers office and said, "How about I take that cab off you today. Ten-thousand dollars, cash."

The dealer stood up from his desk, walked over to Clint, and with great interest said, "Ten-thousand dollars?" Then he coyly looked both ways before leaning in and whispering, "Cash?"

To this, Clint simply responded, "Cash."

The dealer said, "Alright, you got a deal."

This was the single greatest moment of Clint's life. He felt as though everything he had ever done had been validated. Nothing could take him off this high, except for one thing: the money was counterfeit. John Gotti gave him fake money. He couldn't believe it, the honorable John Gotti.

But what was done was done, and now he was on trial. He was getting skewered by the prosecution, until one day, none other than John Gotti busts through the doors of the courtroom and proclaims, "It's alright everyone, he's with me."

At this point the car dealer said, "Oh boy Mr. Gotti, I'm so sorry. I had no idea these were Gotti bucks. I'm dropping all charges."

Gotti turns to the dealer and said, "That's alright, we all make mistakes sometimes. Feel free to redeem those Gotti bucks at a local hitman near you." Then with a wink and a nod, Mr. Gotti coyly stated, "You can use that hit to clean up any other mistakes you've made."

"Wow, thanks Mr. Gotti! I'll be sure to use my free hit responsibly," the taxi dealer giddily replied, notably still in a courtroom.

Then, Gotti turned to the judge and said, "Sir, I'll take this one from here. Clint, you're coming with me."

The two hagglers left the courthouse together. When they got outside, Gotti said to Clint, "I have a proposition for you. I just got you out of some serious prison time. I did you a favor, now you do me a favor. You drive my guys and only my guys around. No questions asked. I'll make it worth your while."

This was honestly a pretty shitty favor Gotti requested, given the fact it was his Gotti bucks that got him in trouble in the first place. But none of that registered with Clint because he had just witnessed the most impressive haggling he had ever seen. Gotti just got him to commit to an exclusive taxi deal that he had no way to say no to. He wasn't even a little mad about agreeing to that deal, he was just happy to witness such masterful haggling.

And he was happy he agreed. Joining the mafia opened up so many new opportunities. He got to be a getaway driver, participate in stakeouts, and even be the driver in a few drive-by's. He no longer lived an ordinary, mundane life. And, most importantly, haggling suddenly became way easier. When he went somewhere with his crew, he could talk them down to practically any price he wanted.

Then, one day, he finally gained the trust of Mr. Gotti, and he was promoted to hitman. His first night on the job he got an assignment from a familiar face: the taxi dealer from the beginning of the story. Yeah, this shit came full circle. The man decided time to cash in those Gotti bucks. Anyway, the taxi dealer, excited to see a familiar face, walked up to Clint and enthusiastically said, "Hey man, what's up! Wow, you've made it big time. Big fancy hitman out here. Listen, as you know, I've got some Gotti bucks, and I want to cash them in. I need you to kill my mailman. Every time he comes by, my dog barks and it's really annoying. Just executing the mailman seems like the most rational thing to do."

Casually nodding in agreement, Clint said, "Makes sense. I can't think of any other solution. You certainly couldn't just ignore the barking that you know is coming. That'd be ridiculous."

"Exactly," replied the dealer.

"Well, I'll have your execution in one to three business days," responded an incredibly professional Clint.

And true to his word, he executed the mailman two business days later. The only problem was that he did a really bad job. His DNA was everywhere. Blood, saliva, even semen for some reason. He was arrested a week later, and 3 months later he was sentenced to life in prison. The guy had no chance in court. He decided to represent himself. He thought he could haggle his way down to 15 years with good behavior, but unfortunately, that court didn't accept cash.

That kids, is the story of how Clinton Fitzsimmons became the chauffeur for the mafia, worked his way up in the mafia machine, and got life in prison for murder. So no, haggling is not a good idea.

This story was brought to you by debit cards. Don't pay cash, use a debit card. Who cares how much it costs. It's just a card, so it's like the money isn't even real. Debit cards, the future's money.

The end.

# SEGUE 4

Yeah, you got me. That last one was just an advertisement. I don't feel bad about it either. Ya boy gots to get paid. Let that be a lesson to you all: there's no such thing as honest art. It's all an act and a steaming pile of the rankest bull shit you'd ever encounter. But anyway, this next tale also never happened. It's something of a fable. Yes, there is at least one message, but don't worry, you won't have to look for it. It's pretty heavy handed. Honestly, you'd have to be pretty stupid to miss it. Whatever, just don't think about it. Enjoy.

# ABDOMINAL CRAMPS: NO LAUGHING MATTER

There was a man named Alan just out walking the streets. He was down in the dumps, but he didn't know why. He was unhappy because that was just the way he was. Although, in this instance he also had some abdominal cramps that weren't helping. Those abdominal cramps were no joke. He could sense that vomit was imminent.

As he was walking, he was met by two concerned strangers, Tara and Jenna. Tara, in a surprisingly folksy tone, said to Alan, "Hey there you old so-and-so, what's got ya down?"

Alan, suddenly ready to just unload on some strangers, replied, "Two things. First, who the fuck talks like that? And second, I don't know what's wrong. I'm just always unhappy. I can't explain it. Every day, every hour, I'm waiting to crash, to be unhappy. I can't explain it. It's like my brain just wants me to be miserable. The only thing I know for sure is these abdominal cramps sure aren't helping. I was out trying to enjoy my day when I got these goddam abdominal cramps. These abdominal cramps are no fuckin' joke."

Tara, in that same folksy tone, because she was just uber folksy, said, "I'm sorry to hear that. And since you seem down I'll even give you a pass for that insult and that cussin'."

"Don't worry, I don't also speak incredibly folksy," interjected her friend Jenna, in a manner which can only be described as not folksy.

Tara turned to Jenna and inquired, "I don't get it, what is this problem you whippersnappers have with how I talk?"

"It's things like whippersnappers," Jenna replied. "When you talk you're just so folksy. It's really off putting. You get used to it, really. It's almost endearing really."

Both touched by the sentiment and irked at being called "off putting", Tara quickly turned to Alan and said, "Anyway, as you can see you get used to how I talk fella, so we'll just move past that." Jenna, behind Tara this whole time, with bugged eyes that exuded emphasis, quickly and dismissively shook her head no, which brought a slight smirk to Alan's face. "Well how 'bout them apples, you're already getting used to me," said Tara, completely oblivious to what was going on behind her.

Alan, now beginning to feel his mood brightening and enjoying the company of these two friendly faces, decided to take a chance and ask to tag along with these two friendly strangers. In response, Jenna, now both pitying Alan and feeling like this depressing motherfucker had some surprising backbone just asking for what he wanted like that, said to Alan, "Ya know, you're really depressing. I mean, holy shit. I am totally bummed out by just being near you. But you have a nice smile and seem like a solid guy. Fuck it, why not. Come with us."

Though normally incredibly shy with those he doesn't know, Alan was thrilled his off-brand bravery led to him being invited along. Though he was excited about this adventure, he was still feeling his miserable, depressing self, so he said, "Awesome! Thank you. I promise I'll try not to be too big of a drag. I mean, these abdominal cramps are no joke."

Tara, irked by all this talk of abdominal cramps, replies, "You don't need to get your panties in a bunch over some abdominal cramps. C'mon, it'll be fun."

On their walk to the bar, they encounter another guy, a guy who clearly has a thing for these ladies, who said, "What up ladies? I see you're looking good tonight. Who's this chode you're out with? He seems like a real bummer."

Tara, just as folksy as ever, replies, "This fella here is Alan. He was down in the dumps so we're trying to cheer him up. And if I may, who are you and why are you speaking to me with that acid tongue?"

This total bro then responded, "I'm Brad, as in I be rad. Haha, nice right? And hey, why the fuck are you talking like that?"

Alan interjected, "She's really folksy."

"It's a whole thing," Jenna asserted.

Brad, annoyed and a little confused by all this, shrugs this off and says to Alan, "So, what's got that stick stuck up your ass."

Alan, in a tone of exasperated defeat, says, "I don't know, I can't explain it. The only thing I know for sure is these abdominal cramps are no joke."

Brad, like a really neat guy, replies, "Abdominal cramps? What, is it your fuckin period or something? Pussy."

Jenna, a little sick of hearing about these cramps herself, interjects, "Ya know, normally I'd get hung up on the fact that this guy just said the worst thing ever, but what is it with you and these fucking cramps? Dude, seriously. I get abdominal cramps, you don't hear me bitching about it."

"I don't know what to tell ya, they're really uncomfortable," Alan responded. "I get nauseous every time I take a hard step or speed up even a little."

Jenna responded to this by rolling her eyes and Brad responded by once again calling him a pussy. Tara, in a commanding, yet still incredibly folksy tone, then declared, "Alright, alright, we're not here to kick a fella when he's down in the dumps. We're here to give some cheer to a fella with the blues. C'mon y'all, let's keep on trekkin' down to the local watering hole."

And on they continued, until they reached the bar, at which point they stopped. At the bar, Alan and Tara talked for hours while Jenna awkwardly lingered as a silent third wheel, because obviously she's an odd duck, too. I mean, her best friend is the folksiest 24-year-old alive. But anyway, back to Alan and Tara. They talked for hours. I suppose it was mostly one-sided. Alan mostly just sat there while Tara said folksy shit, like "whose-y-what's-y," "hooligans," and "a good 'ol fashioned who-done-it." Regardless, they had a great time and clearly had some sort of a connection. Even Tara's folksy way of speaking was beginning to grow on Alan, and Tara seemed to enjoy that she could make Alan smile. It was all going swimmingly until some thief stole Tara's wallet.

"That low-down scoundrel just picked my pocket!" Tara exclaimed, because of course, even in the face of danger, she's still folksy.

Now, Alan was never known as a brave man. In fact, as alluded to earlier by our pal Brad, he was widely regarded as quite the pussy. But in that moment, something came over him. Like someone trying to be a total badass and just missing the mark, Alan defiantly proclaimed, "Not today bitch," and darted after this thief. No amount of abdominal cramping would slow him down. He was a man possessed. With every passing step he gained on the thief. Finally, Alan finally ran him down and tackled him to the ground. Enraged by this man making him sprint with those abdominal cramps, Alan was prepared to start wailing on this guy's stupid face. And it was a stupid face. The face of a true idiot.

But before he could begin his assault, Alan violently threw up all over the thief's face, because those abdominal cramps were no fucking joke. All of the onlookers were equal parts amazed and disturbed. It was so explosive, some of them even felt a little bad for the thief. The lone outlier was Tara. She was thrilled. No one had ever vomited on a criminal for her. She had never seen a man so gallant, so willing to, as she would put it, "exchange fisticuffs in a real kerfuffle." In that moment she knew she found her knight in shining armor. In that moment both of them knew they had something special.

That night they totally fucked. Hard. Tara broke out some S&M gear. Yeah, never judge a book by its folksy cover. Its contents may involve a proclivity for sexual whipping. It's alright though, because Alan liked being whipped. Between that and their surprising affinities for each other's quirks, the two were a perfect match. They would eventually get married and have some of the weirdest fucking kids you'd ever see. They all talked like 1940's cabbies and had intense depression. Because obviously, these two could never just raise "ordinary" people.

But that was the way it was meant to be. They never fixed what people considered to be their shortcomings, they just embraced them and made the best of their situations. They embraced the weird, and as a result, Alan and Tara's lives were fulfilled. And it was all due to one fateful encounter on one seemingly ordinary day. That to Alan, not unlike those abdominal cramps, was no fucking joke.

The end.

# SEGUE 5

I told you that wasn't real. Obviously that would never happen in real life. Let's face it, that guy probably would've just closed his eyes and walked into an intersection. Bam. Story over. Plus, who is that folksy? It's so silly. Now getting back to reality, do you remember Steve from earlier? The guy who developed a superhuman ability to create bold flavors after his plane flew over Chernobyl? Well this is a tale of another passenger on that flight. This is "Ex-Men: Economy Plus."

# Ex-Men: Economy Plus

The dangers of the area surrounding Chernobyl have been known for quite some time, but it had never occurred to most people that exposure to its toxic, radioactive air may provide positive outcomes. But one fateful day, that plane flew over Chernobyl. Sure, a lot of people just got cancer or a superhuman ability to bleed out of their pores, but a handful of passengers developed real, superhuman mutations. They ranged from strength to speed to, yes, flavor creation. Most people who got powers, however, did get more untraditional abilities. In fact, almost everyone got really shitty ones, like Darren, who developed superhuman yodeling ability. Though it admittedly wasn't all bad. He made like 200 bucks off it and never once bled out of his pores.

But you get the idea. No one else really got anything as cool and unique as Big Flavor Steve, except for one unexpected passenger. His name was Chester, Chester David McLaughlin, and he was a dog. He was the handbag Pomeranian of one Lucille Ophelia McLaughlin, who I won't go into detail on because she's largely irrelevant to the story. All you need to know is that she was really into everything being "posh". One morning, Chester awoke from the most Gucci of post-flight, handbag slumbers and just started talking. He walked into his dog mother's room, on his hind legs of course, and said, "Madame Lucille, I need to make poops." She was blown away, flabbergasted, surprised. Her dog talked! It was unbelievable. She also couldn't believe her dog's first words were about making poops. It was so not posh.

But he was a fancy dog with a fancy life and fancy tastes, so naturally it didn't take him long to start talking like a fancy dog. He really learned about how to fit into high society. Chester the Pomeranian began having opinions on which years of wines were drinking nicely and how they paired with a duck confit. But above all else, just like his dog mom, he started saying posh a lot, specifically in reference to things that were decidedly not posh.

And everything was going great. He fit in snug as one of O.J.'s gloves at the yacht club, the wine club, and even his dog mother's renaissance era erotic book club. It's a small, but saucy collection of readings. But one area where he really found himself thriving was dog shows. Chester's dignified nature and his classy, two-legged walk made him an unstoppable force on the dog show scene. He cleaned up, sweeping all the major dog shows in North America and Western Europe.

All his success on the dog show circuit and the fact that he was a talking dog was enough to get him on all the late shows. "The Tonight Show," "Late Night," "The Late Show," "The Late Late Show," and "Conan." He even hosted "Saturday Night Live." And he went on those shows and displayed the greatest volume of poshness ever seen in a dog, even among other handbag Pomeranians.

But it was in this time when he recognized a societal dissonance. While he was beloved by his fellow high society comrades, he grew more and more disliked every time he appeared before the American people. Everyone who Chester the Pomeranian deemed to be "not posh" just thought Chester was snooty. America couldn't stand him. It was an entire country of people that just hated this dog.

This never bugged Chester. He was a dog who never concerned himself with the whims of those he called, "the poors." He thought they were all just jealous because they weren't as posh as he was.

Okay, and this is just a quick aside: for what it's worth, Chester was a total asshole. America was not wrong on this one. He was one snooty, douchebaggy Pomeranian. I hated him with the fury of a thousand suns. I could not fucking stand that obnoxious, money grubbing, fluffy windbag.

Anyway, back to the story. This widespread loathing never got to Chester…until it did. The one thing that ate away at Chester was that the other dogs began to see him differently. He just couldn't relate to them like he used to. Don't get me wrong, he could still communicate in fluent dog. I mean, he could "bow-wow" with the best of 'em. That wasn't the problem. His immersion into high society just made him a little too snooty to relate to his canine companions. And this really stung Chester, for at his core, he was still just a dog.

Chester grew increasingly lonely and restless. Ostracized from the dog community, he never had any playmates with whom he could let out any of his playful energy. As much as he tried to repress it to maintain his fancy facade to all his posh friends, he could never fully stifle the fun-loving pooch blood that flowed through his veins. The more Chester the Pomeranian enveloped himself in this posh persona, the more difficult he found it to really be his fully actualized self. It got to the point where he wasn't even sure if he knew how to be a dog anymore.

His lone doggy vice was a stuffed cockatoo he had. It was named Kristofferson McSqueaks, because, though it was a squeaky toy, it was still posh. He was never allowed to have it out around others because Lucille, his dog mother, in case you forgot her name, thought it wasn't posh to play with toys in the presence of others. So he hid his toy, and with it, the last remnants of his canine identity.

But even though he often had to hide it, he clung to this toy with all his might. It went everywhere with him in that posh-ass Gucci bag. No matter where he was, if Chester was in that bag, he always had one paw on Kristofferson. Kristofferson went everywhere with Chester, because Chester couldn't lose that stuffed cockatoo. Because, deep down, he knew that if he lost Kristofferson McSqueaks, he'd lose what little bit of that dog spirit remained within him.

One day, at the dog park, Chester, as usual, was off by himself playing with his toy, when one dog, a small white dog with a big brown spot, walked up to him. Chester was used to dogs walking up to him. They typically came up to him to let him know he was a snooty asshole. He had become so emotionally calloused that this incessant belittling just rolled right off him at this point, which only made the other dogs more convinced of his immense snootiness.

But this dog was different. Chester could see it in his face. It was like this dog could really "see" him, you know? This dog's name was Spot, ya know, because he had a big spot. When Spot got over to Chester, Spot said, "woof woof bow-wow ruff," which loosely translates to, "Hey Chester, wanna play?"

To this, Chester, with a voice wrought with innocence, replied, "rrr-ruff", which more-or-less means, "Really?"

Spot then flatly and kindly replied, "woof." And then two went off and played with each other.

The two of them played for hours. And it was a real, joyful play. Money, class, and poshness mattered not to the two dogs. Not even to Chester, who knew there was no way Spot was posh, because Spot is a poor dog's name. They never once thought about the other's social standing because how wealthy one dog is relative to another is totally irrelevant. Money didn't dictate their friendship, playfulness did.

From that day on he never allowed himself to be consumed by a meaningless quest for status. Chester dedicated his life to spreading his message that both dogs and people should embrace all of who they are and that money and class don't define who we are. He significantly repaired his image when he did that tell-all interview on "Conan". Chester the Pomeranian really won everyone over with his monologue where he said, "I was raised to think that poshness was akin to greatness. But I see now that this is but a falsehood. I now see that poshness is often a byproduct of nothing more than living in a household with extravagant amounts of wealth. I now see that other dogs and people don't have it as good as me and I was lucky to be that one-in-a-million pup brought into a millionaire family. I may be a talking Pomeranian who sleeps in a Gucci handbag, but I now see that I am no better than any middle class dog who sleeps on a couch.

"I also now see that I don't need to adhere to this capitalist ideal that lauding one's money and status is somehow supposed to make one superior to others. Don't get me wrong, I still enjoy the finer things in life. I won't lie to you. I may still be just another talking Pomeranian, but I still love fine dining and exclusive, pop-up art galleries. I like these things, and I will continue to indulge in them because I like them, but I won't let these things define me or my perception of any other dog for the rest of my days. We should all strive to never again deride anyone on the basis of money or status again."

And some real societal change really did come from this episode of "Conan", because while people will never listen to a human, they will listen to a talking dog. Billionaires began sharing their immense, unspendable wealth with the billions of people less fortunate than them, global famine ceased to be a problem, and poverty and crime rates dropped drastically. And all of this goodness can all be traced back to one lonely talking dog who found a friend.

The end.

# Epilogue

Well, wasn't that fun? That's it. That was my last story. A talking Pomeranian's journey to self-actualization, and how allowing himself to be who he really is opened him up to the companionship that was missing from his life. And that bit at the end, too. My god, to think all it took for billionaires to stop hoarding all of the world's wealth and breaking the global economy was one talking dog. In a way it's almost like the Chernobyl disaster was the best thing to happen to this planet. The world really is an interesting place.

I'm wrapping up now, but I'll leave you with this: if you got any broader message out of this collection of stories as a whole, let it be that you should accept yourself for exactly who you are. Never be afraid of being who you are and doing what makes you happy, because there's always a place for you somewhere.

Well anyway, I've been Ryan, and this has been the story of a bunch of people's lives. Please come back if I ever feel like talking more.

The actual end.